Robert's Short Stories

Ten Family Stories

Robert D. Porter

authorHOUSE®

AuthorHouse™ LLC
1663 Liberty Drive
Bloomington, IN 47403
www.authorhouse.com
Phone: 1-800-839-8640

Published by AuthorHouse 04/30/2014

ISBN: 978-1-4969-0611-3 (sc)
ISBN: 978-1-4969-0737-0 (e)

Library of Congress Control Number: 2014908187

Outside my back window

Sitting in my apartment, sometimes I look out my back window just too see what kind of things are roaming around. One evening, a little excitement came over me when a coyote came around. As fierce as they are supposed to be, it kept traveling on not really paying any attention to people around it. It never attacked any one and like most animals it was just looking for food.

I could say the same about the Deer that show up here once in a while. As far as I can tell, it is a mother Deer and her three children. Cannot tell if they are female or male deer but they are assured a meal of some kind. People put out food for them. One lady has put a salt lick out for them or maybe it is made of sugar. That would be better since salt makes you thirsty all the time. This is my third year at the apartments and I know that for at least two years the deer come back.

Sometime a resident has a party and I set at my window and listen to their music. I never join the parties. One evening it was a scary evening. The weather was strong winds. I was waiting for them to blow out someone's window. Never did though. After 3 years of residence at the M and L Gabriel apartments on Shiloh Springs Road Trotwood Ohio. I have meet up with a lot of people. With a title like Outside My Back Window, people are expecting something evil. Like a witch flying around on her broom, a woman getting raped, people being cracked with whips to do a task of some kind. Not happening. M and L Gabriel apartments are just like all others apartments. People renting them then going on about their business or at least some are going on about their own business. Some are just downright nosey, rainy days and nights.

Some time I set hear just listening to the rain splatter up against my back window. My room is not that big. In fact the back window I am referring to is the only window I have? Not much going on in such a small place. Some time though I think of scary movies I have seen on my old 24 inch television set to keep myself from being bored I write stories. Some thing I learned to do in my younger years. No one ever reads them. But I insist on writing them. I kind of have a dream of being published.

I have even taken classes on writing. Maybe I do it on purpose. You get in your own writing style. Mine is third party writing. I am either the person telling the story or I am an observer translating what is happening or going to happen. Being the third party kind of gives you control. But that is not my intention when I write a story. It is being creative it is a feeling of for me any way writing something that others might enjoy reading. Maybe that is why I write. None violent and none cursing except for shit or damn it once in a while. Maybe the f word once in a while also or maybe a slip of the tongue with M. f. one every 5 or 6 month.

I don't know what it is maybe I don't know as much about English as I thought. Being the only language I know or do I? Sometimes I miss spell a word like I just did with Language Hold on let me check my pocket dictionary. Webster's almost had it except for the "Language" means of communicating. While I'm looking words what defines writing, Webster's says look under write verb wrote, writ'-ten, writ'-ting 1. form words letters etc. produce writing music etc. to write off a debt. writer noun.

So any one writing any language is a writer. Hell woops one of those seldom used curse words. A young child writing his mother sister father brother is a writer. Anyone anywhere putting a letter or letters on anything is a writer.

Wait you say. What about the person who writes echodao letters I made up as I wrote them did in fact spell a word. But is it a word does not a word need meaning? I would say all words or letters have meaning.

A means one like a hat a car a rabbit A is in my mind one. Dictionary A—indefinite article 2each any one. adjective a baseball a basket ball.

the letter B , b abbreviation born. the letter C abbreviation Celsius or centigrade 2 centimeter(s) 3 century 4cirea(about) also ca 5 Copyright 6 cup's ,for 2-6,c that is Webster's definition of the letter C. I could go on and give you a definition of every letter in the English language. What would be the point of that?

One thing about humans is they like to explore other things whether it be another person or a object? Guess the old saying curiosity killed the cat? But if us, humans were not curious where would the world be today? Just a solid rock of Land created by God for human usage?

So in my illustration echodao no such word? Let's look it up in Webster's pocket dictionary. Oh well echo is a word repetition of a sound by reflection of sound waves. But when I added the 'd' that put an end to it being a word. Maybe if I was creating a new Language it might be a word? Sure sounds like one. And that kills my thought that all words have meaning? Or does it? Echodao is not a word. Not in the English language.

I would be more correct if I said all words in the Webster's pocket dictionary have meaning? So if a person comes up too you and says,' Echdao', you reply same too you buddy? Then go on your way. Myself, I would think he was Spanish or Russian.

Here I go getting off the story. Which is Outside my back window? Well I guess I will take a peak. Looking out my window the first thing I see is a no parking sign. Then directly under it tire tracks. So much for no parking. No chance of me getting a no parking ticket I do not drive. Too bad I miss it. About 20 meters I suppose is the property line. Grass starts getting tall.

After the tall grass trees all around, they look like your everyday oak tree. Maybe spruce. But they are all over. Must be a healthy place to live with all the trees. Lot of ox'ygen not oxygen. Definition in Webster's pocket dictionary. Noun colorless gas commonest chemical element. After the tall trees who knows Maybe wild animals of some kind? I have seen deer and squirrel and coyotes. Some dogs here and there but they belong to someone. Maybe I will venture out and see. Then again maybe I'll leave well enough alone. Might run into something I cannot handle. Like some kind of beast. Maybe wild bores or possum.

Maybe some ones farm with cows and horses? Whatever might be there can stay there. Nothing going on. Let's take another look. Over to the left another apartment complex. Has a swimming pool. Mostly used by kids once in a while adult swims in it. I guess they pay for it.

The day is almost over. At night I cannot tell if anything is happening unless someone is having a party. I kind of hate to mention writing story's a lonely business. Sometimes you just got too sit down and close the world out and write whatever comes your way. I am gate full that my publisher got me too buy a computer before I wrote everything by hand.

Takes me a couple of hours to write 10 page story. But then I never was any good at typing. Flunked it 3 times. Not a fast typer. And when you take typing test, they test for speed. Got me there.

One more peek out my back window before hitting the bed. Kind of quite there is hardly any wind the trees are not swaying no wind. No animals running around tame or otherwise. No people either. No rain smacking up against the window pane. Summer time no snow. On the weather channel cold front coming in from up north. Possibly hail storms.

Day over see what's going on tomorrow after my part time job at the church. Lucky me I have part time job. But not for long one more year then back to employment line. Or maybe after 20 years of writing, I'll finely have a real book. Not bunch of unpublished stories.

Okay next day. Back home from my part time job. Well maybe I should have been paying more attention Hogan, Randy Orton John Cena, C.M. Punk, Triple H and The undertaker. After taking a shower something made me look on the closet door where they were hanging Gone someone had came into my apartment when I was not home and took the pictures. I kind of suspect maintenance worker but then I have left home and not locked my door. But I do not think that is the case now. I remember locking the door a I left for work. I kind of in the habit now.

Well that was inside my apartment. My story is what goes on outside my back window. t the moment. Nothing. A very limited range, maybe the whole back yard is two or three acres if that much. If you have ever seen a movie of a spider or bee or any other insect they have a limited range. It is kind of like being in a box car. Looking out into the wild country side. Or being in a box. Or any closed object. With a narrow window.

As far as a story line like one flew over the cuckoo's nest or whatever happened to Mary Jane or even a episode from twilight zone or any horror flick with Hitchcock Bela Lugosi Vincent price Boris Karloff or a Lon Chaney episode. No one getting killed. The only time someone dies is because of an illness.

Well time to look out the window. All right a creature is in the back yard just outside my window. Not a very large one either. About four inches from the ground. It seems to have a tail. It is eating something from out of the ground. It has thin tiny legs and about three toes. The body is kind of chubby for its size. I cannot tell what color its eyes are look black from hear. Its chest brownish. Darn not a vicious animal. Just a little harmless Robin. Well from humans point of view. But from the worm it was eating really vicious.

Can you imagine being a worm crawling around on the ground either looking for food yourself or just trying to get home? This very large creature too you because you're a worm. Land from out of nowhere right in front of you. That would scare the hebee gibees out of me.

Let alone the fact he is chewing you apart. With every bite he takes. Lucky for you though no matter where your body is torn apart, it still has life and if lucky enough will grow to be another worm.

Well the bird has had its full of the night crawler. It flew away. Perhaps to find a different food source like a sun flower seed or watermelon seed. Or maybe it was tired and returned to its nest?

Well I'll get a drink of tee. Out of soda out of kool aid too hot for coffee Maybe? And a box of tee will last at least 3months. The end of the month and my every two week check and my allotment from my wife's death are all going to be here Thursday, Friday and Saturday. I'll be in the money. But knowing me it will all be gone by next Wednesday. I'll probably spend some money having someone marry my lap top to my copier.

Well time to look out this back window again. Hoping to see something scary happening? Oh, I don't know. An airplane crashing in my back yard might stir up some excitement. Or maybe one of the deers crashing into a car driving around. Why it would be in the back yard? I haven't the clue. Or Maybe a Hunter scooting at the deer is why in the first place it crashed into a car.

One last look for the day before it gets to dark to see. Well after my eyes adjust to the night. I can make out images really, no difference except color. All hair at night far away is black only until they get close can I tellhat color their hair and eyes are and what color their cloths are? I think I will take a break. It is only 4:33 p.m. a couple more hours of day light. I guess I will drink a couple glasses of tee. Green or Black tea .I made both.

Well, a note slipped through the bottom of my door. I'm not cleaning my apartment. Bull I spent the whole week end cleaning it. Not only that when I get home from work I'm tired of cleaning. That is what I do all morning. Clean a sanctuary and multipurpose room at the church. When I come I'm cleaning something the floor dishes bah room.

Back to the story. A storm brewing up looks like. The trees are blowing back and forth. Some are bending. After a 5 min of strong winds it begins too rain. First slowly, then a medium rain then a hard fast rain. It is now raining so hard you cannot see 2 feet in front of you. It's raining so hard that it cracks the window. Have to let maintenance know so they can repair the window.

Well that is about how it goes every day. Not rain. But a pretty average life. Go to work come home fix myself dinner. Then write a story. That will be laying around waiting for someone to read it.

The end

Mr. Gray Squirrel

One rainy night in the forest of squirrel valley Miss Ginifer Quiet Squirrel (her middle name was given a month after her birth. She was a shy and timid Squirrel. And when around other Squirrel she was as quite as a (Da) mouse. She might have been more quite. She was so quiet she would be setting next to another squirrel and that squirrel would not know she was setting next to him or her. Eventually she got over her shyness. Everyone was happy for that. Because they would sometime run into her or forget she was around. There was Squirrel that took notice To Miss Ginifer. A middle aged Squirrel. A Gray Squirrel Named Gary Dean Tray Squirrel. Miss Ginifer liked him also because He noticed her when everyone else hardly new she was around.

After a year of courtship, Miss Ginifer had a baby Squirrel. Gary was happy she was having his child. Marriage was not a requirement in the Squirrel world no matter what kind you were—red brown or gray. But Ginifer's baby was exceptional. He was the only squirrel around that was in a class of his own. An original Gray Squirrel. Others were gray but not original. They were mixed with others. A little red and a little gray and a little white. Miss Ginnifer's son had no genes of his father they all came from her. She also was an original Gray squirrel. Ginifer decided to name her son Mr. Gray Squirrel because there was no other color in him.

Mr. Gray Squirrel was an outgoing Young Squirrel he was interested in the valley and went out to find what the valley had to offer him. His first adventure lead him directly into the wooded area of the valley. Not having a father at home Mr. Gray Squirrel had to teach himself how to build a home? He tried making it out of leaves and twigs. But when the rains came it washed his shelter away. So he tried gnawing out an old tree trunk. That was fine for a while but once again the rain and snow eventually wintered the old tree trunk away.

Maybe a New tree would be better? Gnawing out the older tree was easy. But a new tree was kind of hard because it was new, it was stronger. The older trees Limbs were missing. Bark was falling off and had holes where lightning struck. Mr. Gray squirrel decided that the best place to build a home was under ground.

He thought that he would be out of the rain and snow and he would always be dry. He began his inside earth home digging right where he stood burrowing 5 foot 6 foot 8 foot below ground. He made tunnels all threw out the ground. He had different rooms; they're sometime 6 foot apart and going in every direction. His rooms were couple feet wider and deeper than the tunnels

At first the underground home was a secure home. It was built far enough below the ground that rain and snow had no effect. A nice dry home. Mr. Gray Squirrel was satisfied with his home. He now had to supply it with food. Thief was a farm 3 miles down the Road. He could raid it a couple times and get lettuce cabbage and green beans. But a squirrel's diet was really Fruit and Nuts.

Where could he find Nuts in a forest that mostly was nothing but trees? He remembered a friend of his showed him were nuts grew. But that was clear across town. Getting there was not easy. First he had to travel into a town where there were tall creatures on two legs? He would have to be quick about it. The tall creatures were not alone they had a thing on wheels that would crush him. Not only that the creatures were pretty strong themselves.

Some of them could squeeze him to death. Their limbs were so big? But Mr. Gray Squirrel decided it was worth the risk to invade a farm that had nuts on it. In the Squirrel world nuts were like steak and veal and pork are to human back.

Traveling across town was an adventure dodging in and out of cars and human creatures particularly those who hunted Squirrels. Quickness was a part of foraging for nuts. Then getting them across town was another thing. It had to be done in darkness so they would not be seen.

It would take about 6 trips to get enough nuts for a month. And Mr. Gray Squirrel was in an area where six different nuts grew—wall nuts, acorns chest nuts macadamia nuts. That was Mr. Gray Squirrel's best nut. The coconut grew around town also but that was a hard nut to pull across town. Maybe one every month. Takes almost a month to eat one any way. And the Cashew grew in the area. a nice soft nut easy to chew. Mr. Gray Squirrel liked all kinds of nuts and had a variety stored away in his underground home.

Squirrels also like fruits and getting some was as much fun as getting nuts. The fruit gardens were west where the climate was not as hot and water canals were a plenty. Supplying water for the many different types of fruits—all who demand a lot of water. Peaches plumbs watermelon musk melon grapes white green red and purple all were plenty and well taken care of by local fruit growers.

Secret Tombs and Caverns

Another creature that wandered into the caverns was the bore, a stubborn animal that hardly another creature that wandered into the caverns was the bore a stubborn animal that hardly. In the early days before cars trains buses men traveled the country on horses. Horses were the back bone of travel. Yet in the beginning of time oxen were used as transportation and for farming. In stories about ancient times men dug underground tunnels and buried their dead in them. They were called tombs. It is said that Jesus was buried in a tomb when he was crucified. He rose from the dead and exited his tomb.

Great leaders had their own special tombs. Cesar Mark Anthony, Moses and others had been buried in tombs. Their remains turned to dust. But in their tombs it is said that their riches were also buried. King and Queens, dukes, princesses and princes all took their riches with them to their graves.

This led to the creation of grave diggers hoping to find a tomb that had royalty buried in it so they could rob the graves of their riches. Gold diamonds jade ear rings and bracelets. Or something that was of royalty that had value.

When royalty traveled from one country to another their carriages sometimes had gold lined doors and gold hand railing. When traveling by ships they took golden dablooms as a source of payment for supplies or when they stayed at an inn or some ones home.

When traveling by ship they sometimes were held up by what became known as pirates. These tombs soon became known as crypts. Most crypts were inside tombs. They were the body's protection from wild creatures. Most crypts were buried in tombs ten or twenty layers of one tomb on top of another.

During these ancient times armies clashed and their armour was made of gold or steel. That was valuable. They were robbed of these by passersby. The ancient times have many stories of sorcerers, witches, warlocks and vampires lurking around in tombs.

During this time there was a famous and great storm of lightning bolts and thunder as loud as cannon. The sky was dark some of the time, when it was not it was a fiery red from many years of wars.

People of Clermont began hiding in the tombs left by the ancient kings. But to get into the tombs you had to know the secret passage way that led into the tombs. Before getting into the tombs, you had to travel through miles and miles of trails both above ground and below ground. The trails above ground were full of bushes some were full of thistle and thorns.

There were though trial that were thorn and thistle free. They were very rocky and steep and once you climb the top there were many caverns that led underground to depths just as deep as they were steep.

Once inside one of these dark caverns torches of linseed oil were burned to give light to the dark deep. Causing the bat population that clung to the cavern walls to fly away in number to great to count. Sometimes they attacked an intruder to their dark peaceful living quarters.

A majority of them were only 5 feet. That was the younger ones. The elders grew to be 5 and six feet. Bats were not the only creature that roamed the ancient caverns. Spiders crawled among the caverns. None were poisonous but grew very large, about 3feet in diameter and had legs just as large.

Some time the bat population would seek out the smaller spiders to feed on. Easy Pickens but if a bat was really hungry he would get up enough nerve to attack a lager spider. Not so easy to kill. The larger spider put up a fight and some time with it large legs it trap the bat and the bat would then become the spider's food. Still yet other creatures roomed the caverns.

Wild wolves occupied them in the colder months. The wolves mostly ate the spiders seeing that they could not fly. But once in a while they would use their hunting traits (As the wolf was a great hunter.) and creep upon a bat. They found the bat to be more tasty.

A forth creature influenced the caverns a stinger on its one long arm that darted into its prey. It was called the sting ray. The stinger was fragile enough to kill the spider but at the same time could take out a three foot wolf.

But the bat remained above all because he could fly out of range. Yet a fourth creature roamed the caverns much large than any of its predecessors. The orangutan though not a regular occupant would venture into the caverns. Out of its natural environment, the orangutan even wondered into the caverns searching for food. Even the wolf was no match for the orangutan. It was more powerful and could crush its prey to death. But even the orangutan could not depower the bat unless he snuck up on it. The bats flying abilities kept it out of reach of any creature that might wonder into the caverns.

The caverns became known as the meeting place for wild creatures especially in the winter months; when the cold winds of winter and the thick layers of snow forced even the largest animals to seek refuge in the secret caverns and tombs. Large animals or creatures whichever you prefer to call them wandered into the caverns to get out of the cold. Animals like bears not only brown bears but white and gray bears sought out the caverns for warmth. They became the great hunters of the caverns. All who became occupants of the caverns feared the bears no matter what color they were. But even these powerful creatures had problems seeking out food. They were large and had a time carrying their weight around.

Another creature that wondered into the caverns was the bore a stubborn animal that hardly ever baths. In fact when it does bath it baths with mud. if no mud is around it finds water then gets wet then rolls around in the dirt. Even the rough skin of the bore is no match for the cold winters and it also seeks refuge inside the walls of the caverns.

But like the rest it needs to find a food source. The large animals are no match for the bore. He seeks out the smaller creature as his food source.

As the winter gets colder and colder the caverns becomes shelter for all that might wonder into its walls. Even small ants crawl around in the caverns. It is though the caverns show a caring side and has provided a home for all that enters into its interwalls whether they be small or large.

The end.

Shannon Page

Shannon Page was the daughter of a well known writer Jayson Page who wrote the man in the middle. The sky is a heavenly body. Black stallion and curse the day. He died at the age of 50 from cancer of the prostatc.

But his daughter had learned a lot from him about writing and was bound to carry on his legacy. She started out as a writer for a magazine called The Star Magazine.

She covered stories around the world. Each assignment as news worthy of any story. Stories that were about car wrecks, train derailing, new bank being built and backed by other banks and government. After writing for the magazine for 12 years, she decided to write a novel.

It was called The Colorado River she bought house boat and drifted from the beginning of the Colorado River to the end. She also bought a Kodak camera with a extended lens after taking close ups of the rivers banks and the towns she wrote a story about the giant of all rivers. She had pictures other boats on the river pictures of all kinds of fish and pictures of some damage done by the river. It's a best seller. After writing The Colorado River, she wrote her second book a short story called Kelloge it was about a dog that had survived a number of accidents about a dog that despite all his bad illnesses kept alive because of his love for human friend. It also became a number one seller.

After her third novel called breakfast after 2:00 p.m. she went back to writing for a magazine called Nature. While employed by nature she wrote stories about wild animals one was called the orangutan e, one the saber tooth, one baby tigers and one called the beast of the jungle elephants. Altogether, she wrote 4 novels 20 short stories and 634 magazine articles.

Shannon goes too New Zealand.

After a successful writing career Shannon takes a vacation too new Zealand. Arriving, she meets the Prime Minister Mr. Granger. He welcomes her and shows her too her room. It is well furnished and fits her every need. It even has computer she can write a story about New Zealand if She kikes. She did not bring any of her writing tools with her. But the Prime minister saw to it that she was given any writing tools she needed. While there, she visited the Alps, taking three skiing trips. She was not a professional skier but had been skiing about 20 times. She could ski around and writes about the beautiful country side. She was provided a camera with a scope lens.

Why not since the Prime Minister was supplying her with writing tools. Cameras tablets folders and pens. He even provided her with a guide so she would not get lost. The guide took her too classic restaurants that served the best New Zealand foods. One served goats milk with all food dishes. Macaroni, meat loafs, noodle casseroles and beef dinners. At first she was not fond of the goat's milk but later acquired a taste for it.

Today Shannon is going to travel among the Giant pines. She will be taking pictures from all angles. She will set cameras up 24 hours. Each one taking pictures every millisecond. Not only will they be capturing the growth patterns she will capture the animals that pays visits to the pine trees. She also will capture ants that feed on the sap that eases out from their trunk base. She will be taking pictures of the snow capped country side. She will be taking hundreds of pictures. She'll take pictures of visiting skiers and snow mobiles going up and down the snowy mountains, pictures of the tracks they leave. She also will be interviewing professional skiers and talking to the natives of New Zealand. Getting a feel of what it's like living in snow 24—7.

Although it is very cold some of the locals only wear light over coats and ankle boots. She will be investigating the villagers too find out what types of food is eaten. Some say they eat seals but it's not a proven fact. Most live on fish they catch while ice fishing.

New Zealand, its people, its habitat and its freezing weather. She takes about 400 notes and uses them as references for her book.

With time running short until she return home she gathers more notes. Not having much time left until her vacation is up she gather all her New Zealand pictures and samples for her new book.

After her third novel called breakfast after 2:00 p.m. she went back to writing for a magazine called nature. Her first assignment was tigers. As always she set up cameras with lenses that were magnified. They captured a tiger in action. She had films of baby tigers being born. The mother feeding and providing for them while the father was out hunting food for them.

She had pictures of male tigers while hunting. The careful attack always watching every step its prey took. Tigers were not always black and yellow. Some had no stripes at all. Some were black, some were gray tiger and some were white tigers wherein n the area. But her book was not about tigers.

II was about the country of New Zealand and so she left the tiger scene and filmed other animals. Like the brown barn yard owl. Owls grew wildly in the Alps of New Zealand. There were plenty of trees they could nest in. With their keen eye sight they could spot a small animal 5 miles away crossing the snow caps.

She caught the owl in its flight soaring gracefully above the Pine forest and the snow covered valleys. She had caught the owl raiding some of the few farms that were around. Her cameras filmed the owl catching a small bird in the air and eating it. Her camera's filmed the owl bathing which put an end to the myth that owls hardly never bath. They bathe daily mostly at night. And she also filmed owls that were brown gray and white and she even had film of a rustic colored owl.

The muskrat scarcely seen and hardly a permanent fixture in New Zealand did exist in the freezing snow field Alps. Its existence was small and was in danger of becoming extinct because of the hunters that liked hunting and eating the muskrat. The muskrat of today is much quicker because not only do hunter threaten them other larger animals attack them.

One of their most feared enemies is the lions. Much quicker than a tiger the lion can capture a muskrat before the muskrat can turn around or even since that a lion is in the area.

There are other enemies of the muskrat that are just as small. The red tailed fox is just as rare but when faced with a muskrat will always prevail. Although some time the fox slips up and the muskrat will over take him.

While speaking of the red tail fox, she captures one and mounts a small camera on it and is provided with another wild animal surviving in cold country side of New Zealand. The red tail fox in search of its existence and survival in the cold freezing snow field country of New Zealand.

Pine trees are not the only trees growing spruce and willow trees somehow exist. Probably because snow is filled with freezing water. These trees and to New Zealand's beautiful landscape.

But trees and animals are not what attract people too New Zealand. The great hospitality of the villagers catering to all the best foods and the best resorts that has luxury rooms. King size beds fully equipped bath rooms dining areas with tables of fine silverware that shines like new.

Just like she did her first novel she did not write the book in New Zee Land but from notes and pictures she published her second novel New Zealand.

The book showed New Zealand fines places and gave New Zealand an A plus In one of the most beautiful countries in the world and because of the book New Zealand's population grew.

Shannon's new assignment—wild animals in Alaska just as beautiful as New Zealand. The Alaska snow field areas in the world has luxury resorts and provides the logging industry with a variety of lumbers Oak, spruce, pine and dead woods grow in the area. Trees that are large enough to get four or five 12 foot logs out.

But this book was not about the beautiful Alaska but the wild animals that live there. Wild wolves as large as dogs, wild geese with large necks and wild horses with strong legs. horses o that are black gray brown white and mixed color black and white, brown and white brown Shannon also filmed the and black white and black. Because of their mixture they became known as mustangs.

Shannon also filmed the horses and their habitat to learn the everyday lives of the magnificent horses. Shannon always had a camera handy. She knew the value of pictures in a story. Each and every one showing different poses. she knew a book with pictures said a lot more and pictures back up what you are writing about especially if you are writing none fiction.

In fiction some times it's hard to tell what is true and what is not true. That is what makes fiction work, making up things that are exciting and unbelievable. Making up adventures that take you on rivers threw forest across desert into ghost towns and the thrill of reuniting with people you care for.

Shannon knew that and took advantage of all opportunities that came her way. She could add adventure when needed. She could add love to a situation and she could set back and analyze a event that was unfolding. She could add excitement and could make a bad happening into a kind of beauty and an event where everyone comes together and has a good time.

So far Shannon has wrote about 7 different wild animals and has taken pictures of them all. But seven wild animals were not all tier were. Around the world, wild animals exist everywhere. The ape the orangutan the zebra the buffalo deer and just about any four legged animal could be considered as wild especially if they were left alone for a couple years.

Shannon's net adventure would take her into Israel her subject being the mountain goat. Although goats are usually grown in flocks by a shepherd some are wild and roam around in roaming flocks. Those are a much stronger goat. Their strength needed to get them climbing up the mountains. Their horns are sharper and longer because they sharpen then to use it as a hunting tool.

Once in a while they do slip while roaming the mountains but for the most part they have a firm grip on the mountains. But the mountain goat itself was not her assignment. It was the sleeping habits of the Mountain goat. Question arose do they sleep in flocks do they sleep in mates? Do they sleep in long periods or short periods? Do they sleep alone? If so when and how long? Do they sleep lightly or in a deep trance? Those were the assignments of Shannon.

First she had to locate some mountain goats. That meant so long to the dresses and skirts for a while bring on the slacks boots tee shirts and bring on them huge cameras with their photo lenses. And from what she has heard about mountain, goats bring on the strongest deodorant made. Because of its roaming and hunting nature the mountain goat ranch with the wild bores the smell of a dead animal and the smell of food cooked badly.

Shannon's first encounter with the wild mountain goat. A surprise to her the mountain goat she first came in contactwith was not large at all. It was only three feet tall and had no horns. It was a full grown goat and it was a loner. Meaning it's claimed no flock as its own flock.

It was a very easy going mountain goat. Some time just standing in a field of grass grassing on 'it. But if aroused it stood its ground and fenced off any attacking creature. She decided she would give it the name of the lone mountaineer. a fitting name for a lone mountain goat

After studying it for 3 weeks she filmed its every move and was provided with the everyday life of a lone mountain goat. She was covering the lone mountain goat she was covering the family life of a mountain goat. Or the life style of the mountain goat. She filmed took notes wrote down mannerisms habits and any actions that a mountain goat took.

The Mountain Goat became the title of the new story she wrote for the magazine. Not a one article story but a month's worth of stories on the life of a mountain goat. Threw her filming picture taking and writing Shannon gave a lot of people happiness. Her pictures of beautiful animals weather tamed or wild put smile on many people's faces.

Off too Baltimore to film the luxurious Eagle. The eagle was the 8th animal she studied. And from the roomers she had heard about the Eagle she was proud to add it to her already 7 wild animals stories. For this story climbing mountains and trees was crucial. For the eagle nested high in the mountains in trees as tall as a 13 story building. Shannon liked a dress as much as any woman but many of her assignments called for gent's men's shirts and blouses. Once again with camera in hand and movie camera in hand and note pads Shannon began her coverage of wild and the free flying eagle of Baltimore.

Although she was filming in the country side her room was in the Radisson motel on the third floor, room 321. Carrying all that equipment up three flights of stairs was no fun either. After two days she rented a storage room on the first floor and took out the days cameras she would be using for the days filming.

She rented a taxi and he took her as far out into the country side as he could. Out among the tall trees. Removing a pair of binoculars she searched around for a Eagles nest. She searched around for an hour then changed to higher pair of binoculars. After about ten minutes she saw one flying south. To follow it she had trained a crow to seek out the Eagle.

As the crow flew sort of speaking it mapped out a rout too the Eagles nest. Once the crow had found the nest it returned the film and the route to the Eagles nest. After driving about 30 miles she came to the tree where the nest was.

She put on a pair of spiked boots and began climbing a nearby tree. Being in the same tree might be a little dangerous. Hard telling what the Eagle would do especially if it was a mother nursing her young. And to turn out the Eagle was a young mother with 4 chicks—three male and one female. But to get the pictures of the eagle in flight the crow would follow at a distance where the Eagle would not see him. She did film the eagle when it was in full wing spread and she got pictures of it feeding her young.

And threw her trusted crow she obtained pictures of the eagle making love too another eagle. They mated in the evening about 4:300 pm. But the eagle did not have one lover, she had many. Hard telling who the father of her young was? Could have been a different kind of bird, maybe a falcon or a vulture they were in the area also? Does the Eagle go outside its own species for sex? Maybe but evidence shows no. The bald Eagle as beautiful as it is in flight is still referred as the most beautiful bird in flight. Shannon also filmed the Eagle building her nest and repairing it.

Shannon's coverage of the Bald Eagle ran in the paper for two months. It was one of her longest running articles. Shannon in her career at the news paper wrote 25 animal stories. The least running 1 week. But in her career she covered special events like presidential elections parades Dignitaries visiting our country and she covered stories about sports hockie mainly. a few foot ball games and a few base ball games. Shannon writing career was forty years long in her forty years s he meet a lot of people some who were so far in the past she could call them a friend she always revered.

The end.

The Outsider

Barry Lark has always been an outsider. In grade school he was a timid shy fellow. He hardly ever joined in any class games. He always was a watcher. The only time he ever participated was when the teacher Mrs. Cleo Dan, Barry took him by the hand and showed him a game or two. Barry ever spoke not voluntarily. When asked a question he would answer if he knew the answer. If he did not know the answer he shrugged his shoulder then sat quietly at his desk.

He was not like that at home. He felt comfortable at home and was more active. At home he did his chores then retired too his room and played his video games. His favorite was Frogger. He also liked family games like fishing with dad jumping rope with sis and the blob. He had sports game baseball basketball, tennis, golf and bowling.

When he was not playing games he was helping his mother do house work. Being a shy child he did not have very many friends. In fact he only had one friend, Ebby

Smith. Sometime Ebby came over to visit Barry they would go outside and pass a base ball back and forth too each other. Ebby had two ball gloves a catcher's mitt and a left fielders glove. They switched gloves after 50 passes then again after another 50 passes.

Some time they would toss the ball as high and far as they could. Then case after it. Some time catching it and sometimes not. They had pretty good catching skills. They not only tossed the ball high in the sky they also passed grounders and bouncers too each other.

Ebbey had other friends who passed the base ball with him. They had formed a team and would challenge other to play against them. They named their team the Springfield Bobcats. They would play after school on the schools ball park. After school was out no one p any attention to the ball park. There were no adults around and no police either. It did not matter if there were police. They never paid any attention to the park after school hours.

Ebby knew Barry had good catching and gloving skills. He could scoop a ball up in his mitt then throw it to Ebby in a instant. quicker than any one on the Springfield Bob cats team. Ebby wanted Barry on his team but. Barry had no batting skills and besides Barry was still a shy timid boy. Maybe if Ebby could introduce Barry to two players at a time he would get over his timidness and shyness. at first Barry said no. Then thought what harm can 2 guys do? He agreed to play with two other boys. Obbey choose the best batters on the team. He wanted to train Barry how to bat. The first time Barry had a bat in his hand he knew he had to swing at it. Out of 50 pitches Barry only hit the ball five times. But those five times were home run hits. Obey studied Barry's swing. He was starting out low about knee high. Then by the time he fully swung the bat was above his head. Hitting from his knees seemed to be his power.

Obbey figured if Barry would swing slower he would hit more balls. The problem was how much slower? Barry timed a fast ball thrown to the plate when Barry was batting. In order for Barry too hit a fast ball he had to start his swing when the ball was 1/4 of the way to the plate. about equil with first base. drawing a line from first and one from pitcher's mound where they crossed was when Barry needed to start his swing. That was bring the bat up to his buttocks. When the ball reached home Barry should make contact. at first Barry could not tell when the ball reached the intersect between first and home. After about 200 pitches Barry had figured out where the intersecting point was. or at least close enough to where his bat would make contact. But the power was only strong enough for a double or maybe a single. How could ebbey increase the power of Barry's fast ball swing? One or two ways Ebbey thought. Give Barry a heavier bat? or attach weight to a lighter bat. Obbey tried the heavier bat. But that slowed Barry's swing even slower. Then he attached a weight that did not make the bat as heavy. Sure enough. Barry's swing was faster when the weight was removed.

Barry's fast ball hitting increased 75% Out of a hundred he was hitting 75 balls. better than anyone on the team. Next obey introduced Barry too two more players. They were slow ball hitters.

John Smiley and Dave Barrett. Barry needed to slower his swing. even though for the most part Barry's swing was slow. it was not slow enough to hit a slow ball. How could Barry slower his swing? He would have to study a pitcher throwing a slow ball. Where would the pitcher start his slow ball pitch? And how long it would take to get to the plate? To be efficient at hitting a slow ball, Barry studied every pitcher on every team they played. He simulated the pitcher swing and practiced until he had every slow pitchers speed and release point. Barry's slow ball hitting was 65%.

The next kind of pitch was the curve ball. At what point did the ball start it's curve? 1/3 of the way half way or 3/4 of the way too home? Once again each pitcher had a widder release. And the wider the more it curved. once Barry figured that out. He became a three style hitting pro. Although not used very much some pitchers threw a knockle ball. The key to a good knockle ball was two things. Both were power. A stronger throwing arm and strong fingers. strong enough to get a ball all the way too home at a decent speed. A third factor was getting it to spin on its way. A fast strong spin was hard to hit. Barry ignored the spin all together as long as it made it too home in a respectful time he smashed as hard as he could and most of the time got at least a double. Sometimes a triple or even a homer. Barry increased his batting skills to a four style hitter. But Barry was not finished yet one more kind of pitch.

The sinker since Barry was originally a upward swinger starting out low on his body and raising his bat as far as he could with power made him the perfect sinker ball hitter. He loved when a pitcher threw a sinker and would stand at home plate and watch the ball sail out of the park for a home run, Once in a while when he thought he had a homer it dropped at the wall. Lucky for him buy the time the left fielder or center fielder or the short stop or third baseman retrieved the ball he was at least too second, sometimes third. But if the outfielder rebounded the ball and had a quick release he only made it too first base because the ball was at second preventing him from further advancement.

Even though Barry was a better than average ball player, he was still timid and shy. He had learned to0 cope with the loud crowds at the ball park but as soon as the game was over he retrieved too his home, where he spent most of his time studying films of ball games. Once in a while a fellow ball player would stop by. He could handle that. But if more than one stopped in he got nervous especially if they would joke around with him.

Barry was not thrown being a base ball player. The pros were looking at him. He was a one of a kind Not many ball players had a five style hitting record most only three style. Also most were either a good defensive player or a good offensive player. Few were good at both and those who are good at both were dedicated to the game of base ball and practiced both offense and defense every day hours at a time. Barry though was what they called a natural. Base ball was his child hood dream. He had no idea that with his timidness and his shyness he would become so professional player.

He was drafted by the New York Mets playing third base. Although his position changed he was still a proficient base ball player. His batting average never went under 378 his high was 402 in 2000. His first year for the Mets his bases stilling was 109 steals his second year he hit 28 home runs his third year runs batted in 133.

After 3 years with The Mets he was traded to the Philadelphia Phillies once again his position changed. He now plays third base. When he played left field he had a quick release and a strong arm. Playing third base his release is just as quick but he don't need as much power. His batting average has dropped a little but that is because he don't play as much. Mostly he goes in as a pitch hitter. Then he plays about 2 or three innings. At the end of the game he hangs around the club house signing auto graphs. His contract was three years. He becomes a free agent. Saint Louis Tampa Bay and Washington are making bids on him. Washington wins the bid and Barry Lark packs his bags and heeds for Washington. The contract is four years. He remains a third baseman.

In his career, he has only been too Washington 3 times once with the Mets twice with the Phillies. Washington remained his pro team for the rest of his career which was 10 years. During his tenure in the Phillies organization, he made M V P. He also entered into the 30/30 club 30 home runs 3o triples. His 4rth year, he made the all-star game and in 6th year he made the all star games. The rest of his career with Washington he made two trips two the World Series.

Barry retired from playing base ball and became a base ball announcer for w z c k radio in Springfield New York. He later became the announcer for Boston red sox. He remained the announcer the rest of his base ball career. Barry had made a lot of friends in base ball and was humbled that he had been given the opportunity to play base ball and be mentioned in the same company of some of the greats, like Lou Gehrig, Mike Smoltz, Pete Rose, Barry Bonds and the player that had almost the same name Barry Larkin. But his base ball idle is fellow named Alfonso Soriano who is the 40/40 clubs best record with 46/41 and did that playing for Washington Nationals in 2o13. Let's not forget Barry Bonds' brother, Buddy bonds.

When Barry was young he liked watching the reds when Sparky Anderson was their manager. He had watched Sparky play before he was a manager.

Brother, my brother

Mike and Robert were brothers. Their father was a horse trader. He started out with 25 horses. He palominos mustangs and Shetland ponies. He traded them for race horses show horses and males for female horse. That was a good living in the days of the Wild West. But Mike and Robert were not interested in the horse trade business. They liked horses and had a couple of their own. Mike had a white mustang and a spotted Shetland pony. Robert had 2 mustangs a female black and a male brown. They kept them on their father farm.

Mike and Robert by trade were rail road men. Ever since they were young, they kicked trains. Both had model Lionel train sets when they were young. They had the Baltimore and Ohio train sets and they had a couple steam engine sets.

When they were in their 20's, Mike 23 and Robert 25 bought rail road engine and box cars. They car was just coming out. Not yet a factor in travel of long distances. The airplane was not a factor either. The fastest way across country was by railroads. Much faster than the stage coach.

Mike and Robert started out in Topeka Kansas, the center of the United States. They began laying track in Topeka. Mike went the western route. Mike bought 200 acres of western Kansas going west. That almost got him into Colorado. Robert layed track 200 miles east. That got him to Jefferson City. In both directions they had to deal with Indians. In fact they had bought the land from Indians; the Sue and Crow in the west and the Mohawk and Shian going east.

It took Mike 1year to get to Colorado. Robert made the eastern route in10 months. He did not have as many mountains to deal with. From

Colorado to Jefferson City they each built train stations. Altogether 23 train stations. Mike bought a Lionel steam engine five passenger car and 10 box cars. Not too many people were traveling at the time. The country needed a way to get supplies across the country quickly. The engines Mike and Robert bought went to speeds of 15. 6 mile a hour ten miles faster than a wagon train. People from the east wanted textiles from the west—silk and jade. The people from the west wanted vegetables grown in the east—corn, kale and okra. On August 21st, Mike and Robert made their first run. Mike started from Colorado and Robert started from Jefferson City. They met in Arkansas, had a couple beers then mike went to Jefferson City and Robert to Colorado. Mike made the trip in a week and a half. Robert took a little longer; his train was 3 miles slower.

The Chesapeake and the B and O were running north and south. Mike and Robert's goal was to build a rail way from the east coast to the west coast. Mike worked on the line headed west. He bought some more land about 300 more acreage heading west. Robert bought land going east. Mike's crew laid the track going west. But going threw Colorado they had a lot of mountain to carve threw. It took dynamite to blast threw the lime stone and the copper in the mountains. Robert however did not have many mountains Illinois the southern end was mostly farm land and forest. Indiana Evansville was also farm land. Robert did not run into mountains until he reached Frankfort Kentucky, a small town of 300 people that was glad a rail way system came through there. It would bring the people—miners, millwrights and builder. That could mean one thing. Frankfort would grow in population. Lexington is not far from Frankfort and was not much bigger. Its population is 1200. Robert decided to take their rail way into West Virginia; Charleston the flat lands were behind mountains came into his path. Mike had made it threw Colorado He took his track too Provo, Utah then too salt lake city at the time salt lake was a booming mining town with quartzes and jade mines. The miners were glad to see a train that meant men bringing fur and cotton too their town. The fur trade was pretty big business and cotton was also cotton and fur would bring a textile for making coats and long sleeve shirts and pants that would keep a person warm in the winter months.

Mikes next headed to Nevada, Carson City cattle country. And they were glad that a train was coming to town. It would provide a quicker way to get their cattle to market and it would mean that they could now do business with the eastern states. Robert has made it through West Virginia. His track would end in Northfolk Virginia. Even though he did not have far too go the Virginian Mountains were no easy task and the wild life was plentiful deer, rabbit, oxen and moose provided them with plenty of food.

Mike would take his track too Sacramento then to Oakland then into San Jose. The end was near for Mike. He could smell the ocean. The new that Robert had already finished his end of their rail road and he was about to finish his end.

Railroad stations had to be established. Mike and Robert had recorded the mileage from one end to the other approximately 8, 000 miles give or take a few hundred. They had crossed 8 states right in the middle of the country. They figured on 4 stations in each state plus two more for the larger states that was Colorado Utah and Nevada. All western states. They also built cattle yards that shipped cattle all over.

Their rail way was complete. But yet had they named it. They threw up a couple names the East west rails, The coast to coast rail way, The Wells Fargo rail way and the united rail way system. They agreed that the united rail way would be the name. They billed as the freight and passenger rail way system pricing.

They had a problem at first how far could you go on one ticket? They priced a ticket from coast to coast $900.00. A ticket across one state $85.00.priceI price for tickets is not all they had too figure. People had too eat while on the train and so did the cattle. For people they priced a dinner at $5.00 for live stock $25.00 for straw and hey, $35 for any meat by product.

Mr. Pepper

John Pepper was a great Magician. So great was given the name Mr. Pepper the Master Magician. MR. Pepper. John started his magical career doing card tricks. He could shuffle a deck of cards with two fingers. He was so good that he could tell what card his opposing player was holding after a few short rounds of play.

Mr. P some called him and would put a card at the bottom of a pile tap the top of the deck and that chosen card would appear at the top of the deck. After learning a variety of card tricks Mr. P. or M. P others called him.

After learning how to make a card disappear then re-appear Mr. Pepper decided to learn how to make other object disappear and reappear. First he tried a common piece of lead pipe, he would cover it with a towel after attaching a string to it he (the string being too thin to see with the naked eye) John would pull the pipe out from the towel with a quick tug. That was fine but now the second part. Making the pipe re appears. John built a small trench in the ground and a table that was hollow in the middle. Once again with a quick tug the pipe would make its way through the tunnel and into the stand re appearing in plain sight.

Mr. Pepper or Mr. P learned more magical tricks. He like most magicians learned the rabbit in the hat trick and like most learned the quarter behind the ear trick. As simple as they were people still enjoyed seeing them done but those were tricks a teen anger learned.

Mr. Pepper was a professional magician he needed tricks more spectacular. Tricks that would amaze people and make them feel happy at the same time. Making a person disappear and re-appear somewhere else was a feat that would leave every one breath less. To do this trick he hired twins. Dressed them the same then put them in different places, about an acre away from each other one behind a simple curtain and one behind a door. At one moment the woman who was called his assistant named Sherry and the other sister named Terry would take their places. Sherry stood beside the curtain and when given the sign she stepped behind the curtain (moments later Terry would step out from behind the door.

As a young magician Mr. Pepper watched other magicians. Sometimes he learned a trick just by watching. Another magician, he also took a couple lessons from other magical people. He learned the trick of sawing a lady in half from the great Merlin the magician. The trick of putting ones head in a basket and carrying it around was simply a large dolls head sowed into the inside of a straw basket. As Mr. P added tricks to his magical feats he became known more and more. The thing about being a magician was a trick also. Being able to attract a large audience and making them believe your tricks are real is indeed an art form. Mr. P needed to add new trick to his magic. To do this he went to a wizard named Harry wizard. Harries tricks were done with a magical wand. He was indeed a wizard of many talents. With his wand, he could move boulders. No matter what size the boulder was Harry's wand would pick up a boulder the size of a house. It could even move a building. No matter what size it may be. A great get together was planned a meeting of all the great magicians of the world. Harry was excited. He not only got to perform with some of the greats. He also got to meet them and perhaps learn some new tricks he can add to his bag of tricks. Harry gathered his best tricks. Altogether he was allowed 10 tricks to perform; he would start out with the simplest the card trick. His second trick would be the one with the two twins Sherry and Terry. His third trick he picked was the pipe trick.

Each magician preformed three tricks. took a break then preformed three more tricks. While waiting on his second turn Harry (or Mr. Pepper or Mr. P whichever you knew him by.) watched the styles of other magicians. One of his other famous magicians Gallagher, a comic Gallagher would perform magical tricks that did not work. His most famous is the water melon trick. Smashing Water melons with a large wooden sledge hammer. Five more magicians preformed. Mr. Pepper was ready for his next three tricks, each one being harder than the former. Harry's next trick was swallowing three gold fish. Then having them reappear in a gold fish glass container. For real he did not swallow them but cuffed them in his hand and put them in another container. As far as the fish in the container they were always there.

Mr. P gets a new assistant. Connie Franklin was a professional magician's assistant. She had performed with 7 other magicians. She would be a great asset to Mr. Pepper. No doubt she knew all kinds of tricks. She would be bringing along with her tricks from the other 7 magicians. Some Mr. P already knew. Some he did not know those were the ones he was interested in. Connie arrived at Mr. P's two hours early She had a lot of baggage to unload. Not only did she bring her cloths she had a lot of magical gimmicks with her. Harry greeted her at the front office. He showed her to her room Connie thanked MR. P for showing her to her new home. Connie threw gear in the corner of her living room floor she was tired from the long trip. She started out in main here new home was in Idaho. As she had herd Idaho was beautiful during the fall trees were all colors red yellow and brown. You would think you were looking at a Christmas tree full of lights of different colors. On a desk across the half lighted room a clock. She glanced at it and saw that it was 6:20 p.m. Harry had mentioned getting started on their act for Friday. It was Sunday; they had three days to practice. Walking across the half light room, Connie picked up the clock and set it for 5:15. They would start practice at 8:00 A.M. Eastern standard time. They had a lot to go over. She had gotten some letters from Mr. P that told her how a certain magical show preformed. So she was not completely in the dark as what to do during a specific act. She had seen some of Harry's work and was familiar with it.

Connie catches on to magical trick quickly. Given the right props and the right information Connie gets her part right on q. Mr. P is astound with her quick learning. Usually it would take about a month for his other assistance to learn his work. Connie showed Mr. P a couple new magical tricks. Time came closer they were one day away from the show. Connie and Mr. P worked together packing the 14 foot semi. They had a lot of pops to load onto the truck. They also had a lot of different costumes. Different act required different clothing. Connie made sure they were packed right Mr. P had one more trick to teach Connie it was a simple trick with only four parts. She had no trouble and caught on as quickly as she did learning a larger trick. Connie and Mr. P had been a match every since they meet. Connie made the hardest of tricks simple. Most were simple any way.

Opening day

Opening day. Mr. Pepper and Connie were introduced as the magical acts of the Mr. Pepper and Connie magical show. Their first act was a man sawing woman in half. Second act was fish disappearing and a third act was a disappearing auto. Before the fourth act a break, quick snack during break. While on break they went over their next 3 acts. The snake act where Connie let three cobras, that had been trained since they were born to crawl around a person's body without crushing it. The second act of second act was the twin act they were still a pat of Mr. Peppers show. They traveled from main to be a part of the show. The third act was a hard act with 10 steps each step contributed to the next step. Missing a step would be a failure of the whole act. This act took 3 hour to preform and proved to be entertaining from beginning to end. Break again. Since the third act took so long break was an hour instead of half hour.

The finally

The most exciting of al with wizard type tricks, things floating in air with the wave of a wand. Rays extended from wand and crushed rocks they also made things float in the air. Tables, chairs and people floated around like stars in outer space. Just because an object was solidly fastened to ground or building did not matter. The wand would crush it to pieces. The finally was the longest taking four hours to perform. An exciting show that left the audience glad they went to see the show.

The Departure Back Home

Packing the semi was not as hard as it was when they started out. Some of their magic was once used that was it On their return home the semi was only 3/4 of the way full. If it were not for a couple things they acquired it would have been even easier to pack. Mr. Pepper hired a driver to drive the equipment back home. Connie and Mr. P took a train home it was the old Baltimore and Chess a peek. A classic in its day, it took them three days to reach home stopping in Casper Wyoming Sioux Falls North Dakota Milwaukee Wisconsin, Grand Rapids Michigan Cleveland Ohio then home to Buffalo New York. While in Grand Rapids they went to the Grand motel played some poker and Gin seven card stud and roulette. Together they won $600.00 they split it $300 a piece. Also while in Grand Rapids they bought a ticket for a lottery but lost. The train departed Gran rapids at 12:00 AM as the train moved forward to Cleveland Ohio it picked up speed from the hills of Michigan. Entering Cleveland the train station was close to Lake Erie. While there they rented some fishing gear (the train had a layover for the night.) MR. Pepper and Connie caught 5 fish among them. She caught two a Carp and a Bass. Mr. Pepper caught 3 fish 2 carp and a Blue gill.

Pulling into Buffalo

The Baltimore and Chess a Peek pulled into Buffalo, New York on October 21 at 3:00 AM Mr. Pepper lived on the south side, about 40 miles from Buffalo. He lived on a ranch style home. Raised cattle but not for food. He had buffaloes and steers. They lived together did not matter to them that some were cows and the others buffaloes.

To Mr. P animals were sacred. They were put on earth to feed mankind but he never ate one unless it had passed and then only within a couple of days. Mr. Pepper went to his house and Connie to hers it

43

was assigned to her by Mr. P for being his assistant. Her home was not a 4 bed room house with 3 baths and two kitchens. Hers was two bed rooms, one kitchen and two bath rooms. She had two bed rooms for when she had company or a relative visited her.

Mr. Pepper went straight to the bath room and took a shower. Riding on a train was hot and made him sweat. Mr. P. finished his shower. Then set in his den reading the news paper. Read the political page he was a devoted democrat. No matter whom the person was running on democratic ticket he always voted for them even if he did not care for them.

The new magic for the new times

A far more advanced than when Mr. P was learning magic. Mr. P had learned magic mostly by learning from other magicians. Now magic is done by computers and space age technology. Every since the invention of television magic has been a task but Mr. P likes to keep up on the latest magical tricks. He adapts to the new age magic and welcomes it into his bag of magical tricks. If some performs magic on him he cannot get mad lord knows he has performed his magic on others. Mr. P is well known in the magical kingdom and is welcomed around some of the best around. As well Connie is known among magicians as a great assistant and any master magician would be glad to have her assist them whether it be a male or female.

The end

Sinclair, the Bold Eagle

Sinclair was born in a Eagles nest on top of Mount Rushmore his mother a had a three foot wing span and weighed 88 pounds. His father had a 5foot wing span. When flying they glided through the air like feathers floating. Both had great vision spotting an inch worm from high in the ski. Their home nest was straw packed into a mountain. At the time of Sinclair's birth there were three other eggs in the nest. They hatched three days later. They were girl birds. They were named Mia and Shelly. As the young chicks grew they were getting too big for the nest. They had to find nest of their own. Mia and Shelly remained together and built a nest about a half mile from their parent. It was twice as big and built out of wild bushes.

Sinclair remained with his parents another year. He had to find his own food though. Sinclair was getting restless he was three years old and had only flown three miles in either direction. After resting over night Sinclair decided to take his long flight. Sinclair had no idea where he was going or what direction he wanted to fly. He decided to fly south. But he needed to remember where he came from. So he marked his flight by chewing the bark of trees. If there were no trees he would stack rocks or make scratch marks. Sinclair took flight gliding as far as the wind would take him. While in flight, Sinclair made contact with another Eagle HI am great eagle mind if I fly along side of you?

No, I do not mind I could use the company. Flying side by side Sinclair and great eagle headed south where you headed? Great Eagle asks. Not for sure Sinclair replied. Just flying south. Well why don't you come along with me? Where you headed? I am headed to Eagles bluff.

What is that ask Sinclair? It is a place where Eagles meet and have an eagle feast.

After all the Eagles had their party in the vacant field they each flew their separate ways. Mr. Sinclair the bold eagle and Mr. Great Eagle saw the flashes of the cameras bulbs. They were scared by the flashes and flew away. This time they flew south east. The mountains were quite higher in the south east. Mr. Bold Eagle and Mr. Great Eagle had to flap their wings much faster to get over the mountains.

Mr. Bold Eagle and Mr. Great Eagle parted ways. They had returned back near where they first meet. Mr. Bold Eagle returned to his mother nest. She was not in at the time. She was out collecting food for herself and Kathy and Sherry. Mr. Bold eagle waited around for his mother to return. But it was not a very long wait. Mr. Eagle came back from her food search.

Hi son. How was your flight? It was great. I meet a Mr. Great Eagle he was as great as his name. We flew around going south by south west. We went to a field where there were a lot of other Eagles. They were different sizes and different colors. We ate food of all kinds. After it was over we headed back home. I came directly here and waited until you returned home. Mr. bold Eagle had super with his mother then flew back to his nest on the east end of the mountains.

Mr. Bold Eagle was exhausted from his southern trip. He fluffed up his feathers then cuddled into his nest. He slept for 12 hours. When he awoke the sky was a bright blue and in the western ski. Mr. bold Eagle fluffed up his feather just as he did before he went to sleep the night before. Mr. bold eagle was preparing to take flight. This time he flew in a northern pattern. He glided around in the sky for an hour and a half. When he spotted a field mouse running across a field, he took a quick dive eyeing the field mouse as he approached it. With one quick dive, he grasps the field mouse in his sharp claws. Before he reached a high altitude where he leveled off, he had the mouse eaten.

A trip to Eagles landing

Eagle's landing was like no other place Mr. Bold Eagle had been. It was all level land, no mountains around. Another difference was there were other types of birds at Eagles Landing. There were blue birds, hawks, crows, cockatoos, parrots and even a Dove or two. Mr. bold Eagle said good bye to his mother then took flight towards the northern ski. Along the way he meet flocks of Eagles some let him join them and some just flew on past.

Mr. bold Eagle touched land after flying several miles. He landed in a field of cashew nuts. He feasted on them until he was full. He also gathered a few to take with him on his flight to Eagles Landing. Mr. bold Eagle flew for another 25 mile before he landed again. This time he landed on a roof top of a sky scraper. There were signs of other birds that had landed on the roof of the sky scraper. Like different paw marks feathers and foods they had left behind. Mr. bold Eagle left a few signs of his own.

He rested on the roof tops for about three hours then took flight towards Eagle's Landing. It was three hours later when he started honing in on his intended target. He landed on the east side when he got their signs pointed to Eagles landing. Mr. Bold eagle found his spot on top of a perch that had been left by previous Eagles.

After landing on the perch he glanced around. He spots three other birds—one a flamingo, one a crow and one red bird. They were gathering acorns and sesame seeds. Mr. Bold Eagle flew off his perch and landed next to the Flamingo. The flamingo was shaken up and flew away. Mr. Bold eagle gathered some nuts then flew away. The landing was quite large Mr. Bold eagle landed on the opposite side of the landing. There he found grapes his favorite fruit to eat. After spending three days at the landing Mr. Bold Eagle decided he had enough of the Landing and decided to fly back home.

Mr. Bold Eagle meets Mr. and Mrs. Maverick Eagle

Mr. Bold Eagle was flying north to Shy Town when he meet up with The Maverick family. They were flying to Shy Town also. Do you mind if I fly along side of you? Mr. Bold Eagle replied. No we do not mind Mr. Maverick replied. Together they flew north. Mr. Maverick Lead the way he had been north plenty of times He knew where he was going. Mr. Bold Eagle followed Mr. Maverick about twenty paces behind. After Flying for 6 hours they decided to land Mr. Maverick landed first. He landed on top of a rock Mrs. Maverick was next to land. Mr. .Bold Eagle landed about 3 feet behind Mrs. Maverick. Mr. Maverick and Mrs. Maverick stayed side by side. Mr. Bold Eagle was on his own. He looked over the area with his extra powerful eyes. He spotted nothing out of the ordinary. But Mrs. Maverick did. She saw two parrots in the area one were attacking the other. She stopped the larger bird from harming the smaller one. The larger one flew away. The little one had a broken wing. Mr. Bold Eagle repaired the wing and the little one flew away. After repairing the wing Mr. Bold Eagle made a wonderful flight to George Town just a few miles away from the landing. He glided into George Town with a friend. They made the journey several times before. But this time was not the same. This time the small journey was without the wind to carry them further. They had to glide with the air from their wings. After flapping their wings faster and faster the air from them provided them enough power to glide them. Upon their arrival the town of George Town greeted them with open arms.

The Great Eagles Meeting

The Eagle event of the year was going to happen very soon. Mr. Bold Eagle had attended it several times before. Eagles from all around would emerge upon the great Eagle capitol of Eagle kingdom. Mr. Bold Eagle had made a lot of friends at the event and some of them remain his friends to day. Casey Eagle was one of these friends. Casey made friends with Mr. Bold Eagle when they were diving for fish in the Acer valley pond. Mr. Eagle had dove into the pond and captured a very large fish. It was so large that he could not pull it out of the lake. It weighed 28 pound and was 5 foot in length. Not only did the weight make it tough to pull out of the lake but the scales were sharp as razor blades. But one place on the fish's body was free of scales. It was this place where Mr. Bold Eagle was able to take a hold. And the other side was where Mr. Casey was able to take his hold. Together their hold was strong enough to pull the fish out of the pond.

The pond was not the only exciting place at the great Eagle event of the year. The apple orchard was a great place. It had all kinds of apples. Red ones yellow ones green apples. It had Washington Delicious Jonathan and Perkins apples. The eagle likes apples especially the green variety. And collecting all the apples one could collect was the name of name of the game whoever collected most apples won.

The littlest Eagle

Most of the time, the Eagle is the biggest bird around but not in this case. Conley was the smallest Eagle at least in the town of Greenville Conley was only 2 foot and only weighed 4 pounds that was small for Eagle. But his small size did not keep him from being the best Eagle he could be. Conley could do anything a full size eagle could do. Conley challenge larger birds not just Eagles. He could flip his wings just like a humming bird. His nick name was hummer. Conley became a friend of Mr. Bold Eagle and when hummer got in trouble Mr. Bold Eagle would take up for him. And when Conley could not carry a large item Conley would ask Mr. Bold Eagle for help. Conley would do whatever a normal Eagle done but he would have to do it twice. That is where he made up for his size. Conley flew around with little birds. Even though he was an eagle he sometimes felt like a humming bird or a parrot or a sparrow. Sometimes he felt like he was a sparrow. Conley wanted to be like larger Eagles. He wanted to live in an Eagle's nest but it was too big. Conley wanted to be able to spot a prey from miles away then swoop down and pick it up with his claws without even landing. But most prey that Eagle swoop down on are large mice or a baby deer. Even a small mouse was to large form Conley. Conley was not good defending himself either. Other Eagles especially a large one would make fun of Conley's small size.

At first it bothered him; an Eagle is supposed to be a great hunter. But Conley hunting skills were from that of a great Eagle. He could hardly pick up a piece of straw. But Conley made up for his lime of defense. First by flying by him instead of with other Eagles then him by avoiding a conflict by staying out of the normal habits of a great eagle. Also he hung around with Sinclair a lot.

Sinclair joins the Eagles club

Sinclair liked to hunt a lot and that is what the Eagles club did. The Eagles club was formed for older Eagles that did not hunt as much as a younger eagle did. Its present attendance is 50 Eagles. Ranging in size. The Eagles Club was a private club. Only older Eagles could be a member. Sinclair made the 51 member. They had meetings 3 times a month. At the meetings they planned hunting activities. Besides their meetings the 51dmember team would hunt 3 or four times a week. Sinclair's first hunting adventure with the Eagles club was a 25 mile search for prey event. The 51 man team would split up into groups. Each group assigned a special hunt. Some were assigned the task of hunting rabbits some Eagles other birds some other things like a small mouse or a little bug. Sinclair was assigned to bring back ants. A tough job spotting a small aunt from 50 mile was not as easy now that Sinclair was over 40. His eye sight was not as sharp and his speed was getting slower. But Sinclair meets his assignment and brought back some aunts. They were different kinds of ants, red ants, black ants, large small aunts. His tally was 43 aunts collected. They were frozen and saved for later meals. Sinclair had a good hunt and was looking forward to another hunt.

Sinclair meets Betty

Sinclair was on a routine flight when he saw beautiful eagle flying in the same sky as he was. At first he thought it was a male because it was showing male characteristics. Then when it landed it glided into a landing.

Mr. Sinclair was tired from flying around all day. He had to take a break. He went to his nest and took a nap. He slept for four hours. When he woke up, he felt rested. After his little rest, Sinclair decided to take to the ski. He flew east this time. After soaring in the sky for two hours he landed in a golf field. On his way to the ground a golf ball just missed him.

As he set in the green of the 12th hole, golf ball came towards him. Finally the people playing golf chased him away. Mr. Sinclair the Bold Eagle he was disappointed when he was chased off he could not fly straight. His balance was out of proportion. It took him 3 hour to get back on course. When he did get back on course he head further east. He flew another 5 miles then ended in a field of cat tails. It was summer and they were ready to bloom the thistles stuck to his clothing from the cat tails Mr. Sinclair the bold eagle scratched the cat tails off with his beak. Finely after an hour of cat tail removal Mr. Sinclair was able to pick away every thistles he could fine.

Mr. Sinclair flew around in the sky searching for a mate. He was lonely after a couple years of not having any female companion ship. He flew into a crow of women Eagles.

But he was not compatible with any of them. He made friends with a few and went out n dates with them. Mr. Sinclair still lonely took to the sky again searching for a mate. He was flying in the area of Baltimore when he met up with Sylvia. Sylvia was a beautiful eagle that was very smart. She was a expert flyer logging in 5 hours a day in the sky.

Mr. Sinclair was falling in love his heart beat faster every time he saw her. Sylvia was attracted to Mr. Sinclair also. One evening Sylvia was flying in the same air space as Sinclair. She managed to get close to him. When Sinclair dove she dove when Sinclair spread his wings out. She spread hers out also. When he sped up so did she. Sinclair wondered what was going on. He flew closer to her then asks why she was mimicking him? She said it was because he wanted her to notice him. Well it worked he said because we are here together. Hall we have a date? Okay Sylvia said.

The next day they were flying around the sky together. Also the next day they had trips together. And the next finely they became a couple. They dated for about two year going on trips together. Sylvia and Sinclair finely tied them did the Eagle marriage and Became Mr. and Mrs. Sinclair Eagle. .

The Sinclair's first years

Sinclair made a nest in the Rocky mountain area. On the cliffs high above the valley their nest was a five star nest. It had everything an Eagle's nest could have.

Mrs. Sinclair had her first batch of eggs; four altogether—two male Eagles and two female Eagles. Mr. Sinclair named the boys and Mrs. named the girls. The boys were Shayne and Cal. The girls were called Debbie and Rita It was not long after their birth they were flying side by side with their parents. Two years later Sinclair and Sylvia had two more children, Mike and Rose. Rose was the most dominant she took after Sinclair Two years past and the Sinclair's were a fully fledged family of Eagles. They always stayed in touch and flew the sky ways together when they could. Sylvia made sure of that. She never let any of her children forget who their parents were.

One evening Sinclair was enjoying a flight in the sky when he meet up with Dave Cummings Dave was not an Eagle but Lark that Eagle back ground. His father was an eagle. He taught Dave some Eagle traits. His mother taught him his Lark traits. Dave was more of a Lark than an Eagle He mostly hung with mother's side. Larks were not as fast as Eagles But very similar in other ways. They were both great hunters. A Lark's vision was not as great but a Lark had no problem seeking out his prey.

The Larks eating habits were similar but the Lark favored a fruit diet. The Lark lacked matting skills the Lark much rather spend his time hunting.

Sinclair and Sylvia were working on their new home. Sinclair searched around for the best bark he could find. he found a old maple tree that had the bark peeling of it. it had plenty of bark enough to build a three layer nest. Mrs. Sinclair was designing the inside of the nest she use maple and peach for the bed rooms. For the bath she used perch and for the living quarters she used cedar. It took them three month to complete the nest. Sinclair made the nest strong enough to with stand the strongest of winds. He made thick enough to last a long time. Sinclair and Sylvia's new home was a sturdy nest and all the birds in the area admired what Sinclair had done. Whenever their Eagle friends visited they always commented on the fine job the Sinclair's did building their new nest.

A vacation in the south

It was summer time and Sylvia and Sinclair liked to fly down South during the summer months. They did not always fly the same route. Sinclair had made a map of places they had traveled to in the south. Sinclair's favorite was South Carolina. He liked the Evergreen trees and the pine trees. Sylvia liked flying to Florida. She liked the peach pine apple trees. She was not a seed eating bird but a fruit eater. She did eat seed once in a while. Sinclair mapped out their vacation the best he could. He knew that they would get off track and adjusted the map so it would be of more help. Sinclair packed some summer cloths Sylvia did also. They would be leaving at 3:00 in the morning.

The wanted to be in the south by a three day flight that would include the times they stopped to rest and a couple of hours sleep. Sinclair finished the Map. The best he knew. Sylvia packed the food they would be eating. She made sure that fruit was in the lunches.

Sylvia and Sinclair were ready for their trip. After a full nights rest they would start out on their trip. The first thing—no breakfast just a quick washing up then to the sky they headed.

The arrival down south

Sinclair and Sylvia landed in southern Mississippi around the Jackson area. They would spend the night then head out round 6:00 AM. While in Jackson they stayed at the Blue Ridge motel. Also while at the motel they meet John and Sussie Eagle.

They were returning from a southern vacation. The Sinclairs and the Eagles had dinner together. While at the motel, after dinner The Sinclair's went to their room and fell asleep. The Sinclairs said good bye to the Eagles then headed to Florida. The rest of the trip took about 2 hours and before you knew it they were in Tampa bay area of Florida taking a bath in the Gulf of Mexico.

The end.

New products

The quarter Master has new product from around the world. All together 250 new product, too many to mention but if you look one up you will be sure to find it. a couple new products are food products Quarter Master for the first time in its history is shipping food products. This means refrigerated trucks will be added to the form. To accommodate the food industry separate stalls are added so foods are not mixed. Frozen foods are at the front near the cabs in the middle fresh veggies and at the ends are pasta's or any other condiment like salt pepper sugar and spices.

Another new product is clothing separate closets for different types of clothing dresses for women and all woman attire is at front so it will not get damaged . . . Woman's shoe's on the right in padded stalls. Men's clothing at the back with stalls for suites dress pants men's slacks like dungarees folded in bends. Shoes in boxes stacked 15 high.in 24 rows.

Toys are also new wood toys boxed and stacked at front of box cars plastic toys middle of truck and paper toys like games right side middle truck. Basketball's, foot balls and other sports equipment at the back of truck right side.

Merger with airlines

The quarter master trucking firm merges with air lines shipping products across international waters is a big business. The quicker a product reaches its destination the quicker company's make a profit and the happier the customer is for receiving his product as soon as possible. Quarter Master has merged with six shipping freight air lines.

These air lines only freight no passengers. The only passengers is the crew which includes pilot co—pilot and a handy man to see to it freight has as little damage as possible. The freight trucks drive product to air port where they are removed from trucks and stored in bens until a air plane becomes available. Removed from bens product is driven by huge forklifts that put the product inside the cargo area. a smaller fork lift inside cargo plane removes product from larger lift then stacks it inside the plane.

Each product is padded so product will not get damaged then securely tied down so it will not slide around cargo plane also so one product does not mix with another.

Setting on Tuckers desk is order that needs to be shipped by plane. Checking the orders Tucker checks of a list of products being sent to Denver Colorado. They will be delivered to HMS freight lines then shipped to designated area. Air line Coffee Air freight is an air line that only ships coffee. Trucks of coffee will be delivered to coffee air lines where it will be stored in a warehouse. Refrigerated then shipped by air to its destination. A third Air line Morrison air freight awaits arrival of leather goods. Quarter Master will deliver by truck 21 skids of computer paper and computers.

The Decline

With money being tight Quarter Master dumps clients that have slow or low outcomes. They also dump old trucks that are in need of repairs. Looking at their assets they can tell witch firms and witch product is yielding low profits and which ones are costing the industry large losses The balance sheet reflect losses and profits and is a good tool for keeping company's afloat. Being a low economy year for Quarter Master trucking firm, they also lay off hired help but do not leave them hanging. They give them either a separation pay or retirement check. Or even stocks pay outs. They also give them a return to work clause that states they can return to work when economy picks up. Quarter

Master cares about their employees they value their input in company and know that the employee is one of their greatest assets.

The economy picks up.

The Quarter Master Trucking Co. has been in a decline for three years. Profits for those three years were at the company lowest. With the added clients and new product production has built back up and once again Quarter Master rates among the top 100 companies in the United States and in the top 500 worldwide. As promised in their release of employee and some company's Quarter Master has rehired laid off employees and restarted relationship with past company's Tucker is still called Tucker The Trucker once in a while. But it has been 15 years since he has been behind the wheel of a semi. He rarely drives to work most of the time fellow employees pick him up for work. For his great work he has been promoted to chief trucking consultant as a result of the economy turning around. He was also given a healthy raise and added benefits.

The Firm

Tucker's quartermaster trucking firm is growing at the present 1256 trucks are in operation. The quartermaster has taken on 12 new firms and each firm has from 1500 to 2000 working force. The quartermaster will be putting on the road from 1900 to 30,000 new trucks. Each truck will have 14 routes per week. Tucker we be taking part in the management of the added trucking route. From a home base Tucker will assist give direction to monitor and help the new clients. Tucker has been assigned 10 trucks with each truck two drivers and two routes per day will be given to each truck drivers and their assistance tucker is paymaster of all the new drivers. He will log their time amount of products and what they are carrying.

The truckers assigned to the new trucks are Gary Pantry, assistant Mike Rogers, Bob Maverick, assistant James Monroe, Connie Kelly, assistant Gregg More, John Miller, assistant Red Pepper, Shane Cummings, assistant Dian Blackstone, assistant Harry Carry, and Fred Acer, assistant. Jerry Savage.

Every morning at 7:00 A.M. Tucker assigns a trucker to a new route. Also at 6:00 pm. He assigns drivers and their assistants' new routes. The reason they are given new routes is so everyone knows all routes when a driver calls in sick there is someone to take his place or his assistant. Place. At no time is there a shut down. Trucks are on the road 24—7 making deliveries. Tucker still drives a truck and makes deliveries twice a week in the evenings. Most of the time, he is now a consultant to the drivers.

The end.